to
Martha, Pepa,
Daphne, and Maia

Other books by David Lucas:

Halibut Jackson
Nutmeg

THIS IS A BORZOI BOOK PUBLISHED BY ALFRED A. KNOPF

Copyright © 2006 by David Lucas
All rights reserved.
Published in the United States by Alfred A. Knopf, an imprint of Random House Children's Books,
a division of Random House, Inc., New York. Originally published in Great Britain by Andersen Press Ltd., London, in 2006.
KNOPF, BORZOI BOOKS, and the colophon are registered trademarks of Random House, Inc.

www.randomhouse.com/kids

Educators and librarians, for a variety of teaching tools, visit us at
www.randomhouse.com/teachers

Library of Congress Cataloging-in-Publication Data available upon request.

ISBN 978-0-375-84338-9 (trade) - ISBN 978-0-375-94338-6 (lib. bdg.)

The illustrations in this book were created using ink and watercolor on wallpaper.

PRINTED IN ITALY

June 2007

10 9 8 7 6 5 4 3 2 1

First American Edition

whale

David Lucas

Alfred A. Knopf 🐎 New York

Joe was sound asleep
as the waves crashed on the shore
and the windows rattled in the gale.
Until *barooom!*
the whole house shook,
the floor tipped up, and
Joe fell out of bed.

It was morning, but it was still dark outside.
Something was wrong.

"Grandma May," said Joe.
"It's still dark outside!"
They went to the door . . .
but they couldn't get out.

Joe ran up to the attic.
"There's someone at the window!"

Grandma May put on
her Going Out Hat
and grabbed her umbrella.
"Right, come on, then," she said.
"Up the chimney!"

They stood on the roof.
"A fish!"
said Grandma May.
"A *whale*,"
Joe whispered.

Joe and Grandma May clambered up . . . up . . . up to the
top of the Whale. The townsfolk were all there, talking
at once, and even the Owl who had lived in the
Clock Tower was there. The Mayor spoke up:
"O Whale! What have you done? Our town is ruined."
"I'm truly sorry," boomed the Whale.
"I was frolicking in the bay, singing in the storm.
I got carried away trying to balance on my tail.
Now I'm done for. You may as well chop me in pieces.
I would make a magnificent fish pie."
"He would indeed," agreed the Fishmonger.

"But we *must* help the Whale!" said Joe.
"How?" asked the Mayor.
"I don't know," said Joe.

"At least let me ask the Owl," said Joe.

"*Whoo* now," said the Owl. "Let me ask the Wind."

And the Owl flew high in the air.

"He really would make a magnificent fish pie,"
said the Fishmonger.

"No!" said Joe.

At last the Owl returned.

"I have spoken to the Wind," he said.

"The Wind has gone to speak to the Sun.

The Sun will want to speak to the Moon.

The Moon will want to speak to the Innumerable Stars.

The Innumerable Stars will, no doubt, want to talk it over
amongst themselves."

"Then we must wait," said Joe.

And so they waited . . .

It was morning when at last the Wind fluttered in the Owl's ear.

"The Wind has spoken to the Sun," said the Owl.

"The Sun has spoken to the Moon,
the Moon has spoken to the Innumerable Stars,
the Innumerable Stars have talked amongst themselves,
and they are all agreed that we must sing."

"Sing?" said the Mayor.

"Sing?" said the Fishmonger.

"But what shall we sing?" asked Grandma May.

"The Rain Song!" shouted Joe.

"The Rain Song doesn't work," said the Mayor.
"Everyone knows that."
But Joe began to sing, the Owl began to hoot,
and soon everyone joined in.
"Rain rain, splish splash,
thunder crack and lightning flash!"
And then the Whale joined in,
in a voice so big the land shook.

It was only a song.
They hadn't really
expected it to work. . . .

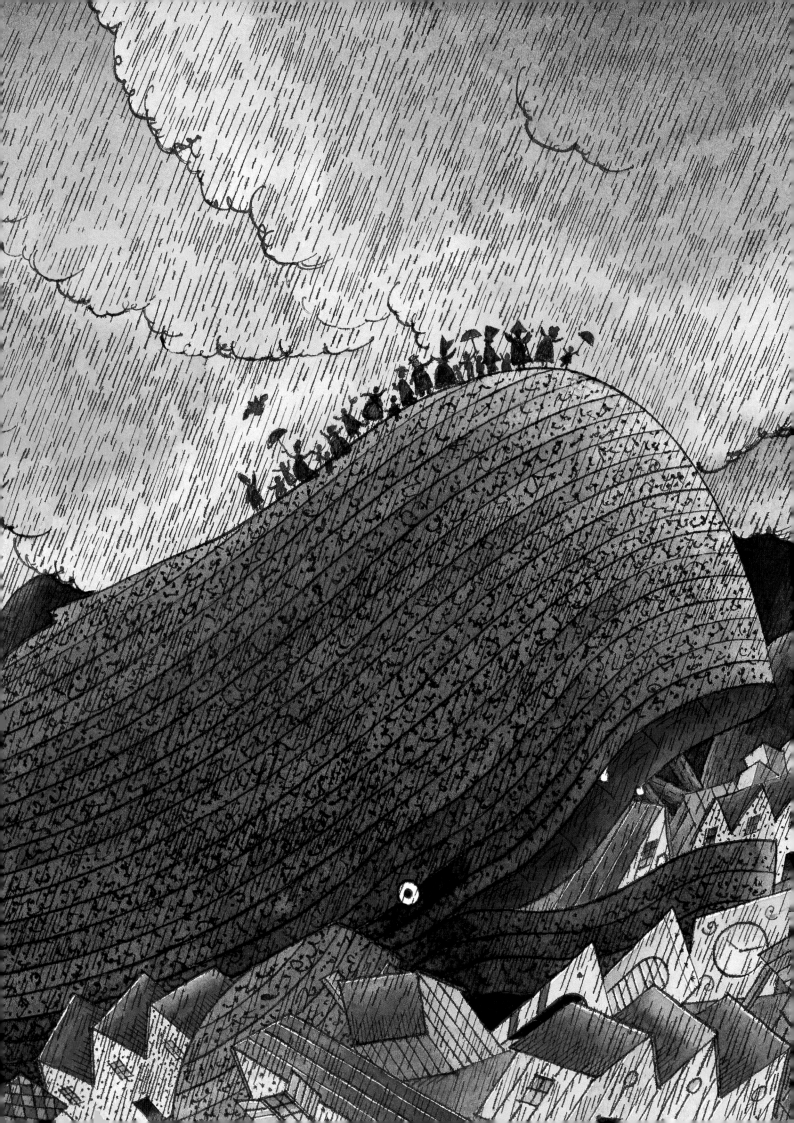

Soon the whole town was flooded.
The Whale was afloat.
"But now *we* are stuck!" said the Mayor.

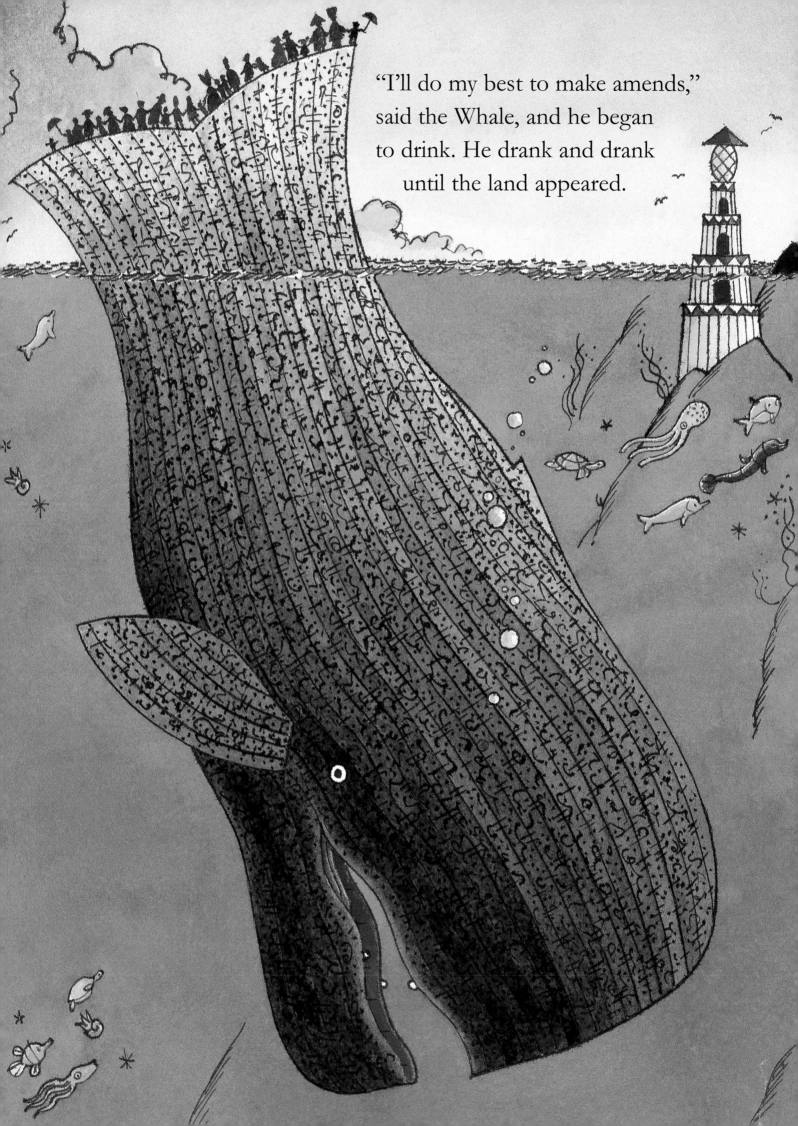

"I'll do my best to make amends,"
said the Whale, and he began
to drink. He drank and drank
until the land appeared.

And one by one, the
townsfolk went ashore.
"Our town!"
groaned the Mayor.
"Oh dear!" said Joe.

But out in the bay the Whale was singing.

"It's fish language," the Owl whispered to Joe.

And every kind of sea creature and seabird came toward the shore,

carrying shells and bright pebbles and pearls.

And an army of fiddler crabs marched up the beach

and set about making the town more beautiful than ever before.

The townsfolk were delighted.
"Thank you, Whale!" they said, and waved goodbye.
"Goodbye!" boomed the Whale. "Thank you, Joe," he called.
"I promise I'll come back and see you again one day!"